SODOM

Kelvin V.A Allison

This novel is dedicated to Lolly, and Jessie.
Love you both

ZOE

"Where were we?" Zoe stared at the bloody form of her neighbour David as the man lay tied face-up over the table that had held her just half hour before.

He had turned his head as she had re-entered the room, his face set with grief and dread as he watched her place the tray that she was carrying on the carpet then met her gaze. "Please, Zoe…please I am so sorry!"

"Calm down," she hushed him, dropping to a crouch beside his face, watching as he winced and turned his gaze away from the proximity of her nudity. "What's the matter David, you seemed quite happy to see my body a little while ago."

He stayed silent for a moment, tear-filled eyes staring up at the ceiling above where he lay, and when he spoke his voice was thick with grief. "I am so sorry…the things I did…oh my God…please…"

"Now now, no tears please, it's a waste of good suffering," she stated, frowning as she realised that she had just quoted a film. For a moment she stayed crouched beside her prisoner, trying to recall which movie, but then she sighed wearily and let her gaze drift over the naked, bloody figure of David. It wasn't his blood, but rather that of her friend E.V. she turned at the thought, studying the headless body that was still tied face down over the second coffee table with disassociated calm. She knew that she should be experiencing shock, horror, and revulsion.

Yet there was nothing where that should be.

It was as if she was a blank slate.

"I deserve to be punished for everything that I did to you…and others…I understand that!" David was crying openly now, tears rolling down his cheeks and as she glanced back at him, she could tell that he was being sincere. "Are you going to tell the police that I am here…"

"Why would I do that?"

He blinked. "To come and take me away?"

"Away?" she shook her head. "No, that won't do. You are going to be staying with me for a while."

"But…" he blinked, his breath catching in his throat as he realised the implications of her words, and Zoe shuddered as she felt the rush of emotion that suddenly coursed through her at his raw terror.

What was it that he had said while he had been torturing her and E.V less than an hour ago?

That he could feel nothing at all except when she was experiencing fear or pain?

Was that how it was for her now?

With disturbing calm, she realised that whatever had been dispersed from the rocket earlier that day and breathed in by the male populace had run its course, only for women to now be affected?

Had that been deliberate on the part of its creator? To let the men cause complete havoc and destruction only to then be replaced by the women?

Or had it been their physiology that had caused the men to succumb before the women?

Zoe stared down at the man before, feeling the smothering blanket of apathy settling about her like a shroud once more, choking the life from her.

On instinct, she reached out and slapped David hard across the face, shuddering in excitement as he yelped in pain and fear, his eyes bulging wide as he looked at her. "Please don't hurt me, Zoe!"

"Why are we doing these things?" she asked him, genuinely curious and strapped to the table, his cheek red from the slap, David blinked in confusion.

"I…I don't know…"

"You said you killed your wife."

He nodded, tears filling his eyes. "I did, and her dog. I deserve to be locked up!"

"She was an awful woman," Zoe stated, her voice monotone. "And that fucking dog wouldn't shut up with its barking. You did the world a favour."

"What?" he started to shake his head. "I killed her, I killed your friend…I…Oh God…the things I've done…"

"It was the dust," she told him, certain now.

"The dust?"

Zoe nodded, catching her bottom lip between her teeth as she studied him. Then. "Are you ready?"

"Ready?" his voice was a sob of fear.

He screamed as she raised the hammer from the tray of items that she had collected from the kitchen and raised it high over her right shoulder.

Without hesitating, she brought it straight back down, frowning in irritation as the head of the hammer missed her target and struck him hard upon the upper thigh, drawing a grunt of pain from him.

She raised the hammer again, concentrating harder this time, and brought it speeding down once more.

David screamed in agony as the head of the hammer struck him hard upon the right testicle, the force of the blow mashing the oval shaped glans flat like a hairy-hamburger before it regained its shape.

The scream was still rising in pitch when she struck him a third time, this one catching both of his testicles. David screeched in agony, his legs bucking against the rope, his eyes bulging wide in his face.

Zoe struck him twice more, the last blow splitting his wrinkly scrotum with an inch long gash and as David thrashed about in pain, she leaned forward, poking at the hole with a long fingernail.

With a grunt, he passed out, his body seeking refuge in unconsciousness as he soared past the limits of his pain threshold, and scowling, Zoe rose and headed through to the kitchen, then returned.

David woke the moment that she tilted the vinegar bottle she had collected from the kitchen, the liquid that she was pouring through the split in his scrotum burning like lava as it flowed over the raw meat contained within. Eyes wide, he thrashed like a madman, and for a moment she thought that he might break free, so desperate were his struggles.

Through it all, Zoe sat and watched him, her breathing heavy as she saw the agony that he was going through, her nipples hard with excitement as she considered how much power she had over him.

Was this how it had been for him?

On impulse she reached out and took his cock in her hand, her fingers and inch or so from touching around the base. He froze at her touch, staring at her through tear-filled eyes as he hissed in pain, and she turned to meet his gaze as she began to move her fingers. "What a big boy you are David. Did Clare like being on the receiving end of this?"

Her prisoner choked back a sob, and she raised the vinegar with her free hand, moving it back towards his scrotum. "I asked you a question."

"No," he howled piteously, head shaking, snot running from his nostrils. "She said it was too big."

Zoe nodded, then turned to study it once again, moving her face closer as she spoke. "You were going to use this on me, weren't you."

It wasn't a question, but he shook his head. "I am so sorry, I wasn't…I wasn't in control of myself!"

"The gas made you do it?"

"Yes!" he nodded. "It wasn't my fault."

Zoe smirked, still staring at his cock. "You were going to push this in my mouth, and my cunt, and up my arse…weren't you?"

His lips moved silently, head seeming unsure whether it wanted to nod or shake, and she gave a soft chuckle. "I've never liked un-circumcised cocks."

"What?"

"Don't go away," she told him, rising once more, and returning to the kitchen. When she came back, she found him resting his head back down, eyes staring up at the ceiling, but he turned at the sound of her approach and screamed in terror.

"Let's get rid of this foreskin shall we," she dropped back down beside the table, the fingers of her left hand grasping the head of his cock and pulling, stretching it taught away from his body. David screeched as she raised the Y-Shaped potato peeler in her other hand, the sound tore from the last vestiges of his sanity as he stared up at the plastic handled tool with the serrated metal blade joining the two arms of the head. With a quick downward sweep of her arm, she swiped at the meat of his cock with the potato peeler, her eyes widening in excitement as an inch wide slice of skin began to slide through the gap in the blade, reminding her of a takeaway worker slicing strips from a kebab on a spit. As she neared his bloody ball bag, the strip fell loose to stick to his legs, and she swiped at him again, removing a larger strip. Blood began to run from the shaft as the skin began to split and fall away, leaving the thick length of meat in her grip slippery and raw. Without warming it slipped from her fingertips and she sighed wearily, tossing the potato peeler to the carpet.

Dropping her eyes to the small pile of slices of bloody meat and muscle atop David's groin, she turned to meet his gaze and smiled. "You made me drink snot, and shit and blood."

He tried to speak, blinking tears away from her as his lips moved in an inarticulate gargle of pain, and she nodded at him. "Open wide for mummy."

"No!" David managed to sob, his head shaking weakly as she lifted one of the bloody strips of foreskin to dangle over his mouth, making aeroplane noises as she did so.

He clamped his lips tightly together, eyes closing as if to block out the sight of what she was trying to feed him, only to scream as she poured the vinegar over his raw, bloody shaft with her free hand.

As his lips spread wide, she dropped the bloody slice of foreskin between his teeth, then clamped her hand over his mouth, shuddering with excitement as he began to choke on the offering.

"Come on, chew it up, swallow it down!"

His nostrils flared, his throat working overtime as he tried to swallow the grisly blockage in his throat, his eyes almost bulging from their sockets.

Somehow, he managed to swallow it, his mouth opening once more to suck in air only for her to push more strips of foreskin into it. "Go on, eat!"

He moaned loudly around the meat in his mouth, and she leaned on his lips with both hands, her face just inches from his as she stared into his eyes, enjoying the terror she saw there as she taunted him. "Go on, eat that cock up like a good girl!"

With a choking sob, he cleared his mouth once more and she leaned back on her heels, bored with this game now, and eagerly seeking a new high, while before her on the table, David clamped his eyes shut. "Please…please let me go…"

"I don't like you closing your eyes," she told him, her head shaking. "I want you to see all the fun that we are going to have together!"

"Please," he repeated, his face screwing up as he squeezed his eyes tighter together. "No more!"

With a snarl, Zoe reached down to the tray that she had carried in earlier, snatching up the craft knife that she had collected along with some other tools and placed it between her teeth. Reaching out she grasped at David's head, her naked form almost straddling his and he sobbed as her right knee bumped his mutilated penis.

The sob turned to a gasp of shock and fear as she plucked at his right eyelid with the fingers of her right hand, holding his head down as her left hand pushed on his forehead. Before he could even attempt to pull his head away, she shifted her left hand to her mouth, snatching the craft knife free and then slashed at the stretched-out eyelid. The razor-sharp blade of the craft knife sliced through the thin skin with ease, detaching the let side of it from his face, and smiling, she ripped the hand holding the eyelid to the side, watching as it stretched then tore.

For a moment it seemed as though the elasticity of the eyelid might keep it attached but a quick swipe with the craft knife cut the sliver of connecting skin away. Zoe flicked her hand towards David, watching as the eyelid, sticky with blood, and wrinkled like a dying slug flew from her hand to stick to her prisoners chest just below his right nipple.

He howled like a wounded animal, his right eye staring out at her in horror, blood running freely into the white orb which without the eyelid looked as big as a snooker ball. Without even giving it thought, Zoe reached out once more, plucking at his other eyelid with her bloody fingers. The blade slashed again, and David's scream took on an almost animalistic edge as he strained against his bonds, both eyes large and bloody as they stared at her.

Chest heaving with excitement, Zoe rose and stepped back from the table, what felt like an orgasm rising within her as she studied the mutilated form of the man tied to the table before her. Instinctively she lowered a hand between her legs, fingers stroking, as she raised her other hand to her chest, brushing against each of her hard nipples with the stiff plastic handle of the blade. Voice monotone, she stared down at her prisoner. "Well, you've got me all wet David, that's what you wanted wasn't it."

He screamed at her, a strangled insane screech devoid of humanity and she nodded, then gave a grunt as her eyes slid past him to settle upon the body of the dog which David had shot in the head.

The dog that had raped her over the table.

She blinked at the thought, no longer feeling the disgust and horror she had felt during the act, her new emotionless world view instead making her realise she had never been fucked like that before.

So much power. So much aggression.

Her eyes dropped back down to David, his words as he had discovered the dog fucking her returning to her mind. *"You've ruined her."*

"You ruined me," she stated, drawing David's gaze away from where he had been staring off across the room, bloody tear tracks staining his cheeks as he looked at her in horror as she continued. "But don't worry, lover, I am going to ruin you too."

She bent back down beside the table, dropping the knife as she lifted the largest item from the tray of objects that she had gathered. He sobbed as he saw it, head starting to shake, and shuddering at his fear, Zoe began to buckle the harness of the strap-on to her body, her left hand reaching out to encircle the shaft of the big silicone cock, her fingers sliding.

She stood for a moment, wanking the fake cock as she held his gaze, enjoying the fact that he couldn't close his eyes to her display. Then she bent and cut through the cords securing his ankles to the table legs. Even before he could react, she grasped at his feet and flipped them to the side, literally rolling the sweaty blood-covered body of the man over on the table, his bound arms crossing above his head.

He screeched as his skinned cock and torn scrotum got caught between his body and the table, and grinning, she stamped on his lower back hard, drawing another piteous scream of pain from him.

Swinging a leg over his back, she straddled the table as she edged herself over his bare arse, the fingers of her left hand splaying his buttocks apart.

They separated with a wet noise, and had she been able to feel anything but excitement at his pain and terror, Zoe knew that she would have felt disgust as she saw the hairs of his arse separate, some of them so soaked with sweat that it looked like cheese strands separating on a pizza, several of which had tiny pieces of shitty toilet paper attached to them like hairy anal beads. To match the image, a strong aroma of hot beefy cheese seemed to wash up from her prisoners ring-piece, and wrinkling her nose in the memory of disgust, Zoe stared down at David's puckered arsehole, a grey and purple snowflake adorned with hairs and piles like mouldy grapes.

"Narrrghhh!" David suddenly tried to free himself, rising his buttocks beneath her, but Zoe grasped at the shaft of the fake cock with her right hand and pushed downwards at the very same time.

His moan of denial turned to a grunt of shock as the big silicone cock pushed inside him, added by inertia and his own arse sweat, the lube of choice for prison rapists since buggery had begun.

The air rushed from his lungs as he dropped back down to the table, and shifting her feet, Zoe let herself drop with him, burying the full eight inches of the silicone sex toy inside his aching arsehole in one foul swoop. Moaning at the effect his pain was having on her, Zoe rose staring down to find that his arsehole had split at her violent invasion of his body, David's blood joining his sweat on her strap-on cock.

Licking at her lips, she pushed back inside him, her hands reaching out to grasp at his hair, tilting his wide-eyed head back to stare at the ceiling, a low guttural moan of agony escaping from his lips.

"This belonged to a girlfriend of mine," she leaned forward to groan in his left ear as she fucked him with hard thrusts. "It's nearly as big as yours David, or what you had…I only wish I could get that dog to fuck you like he fucked me. So much power. So much animal passion."

She knew that she should have felt shame at her words, disgust even at the thought of what she was saying, but there was nothing but the pleasure of humiliating and torturing her former captor, a man who until this morning she had considered a friend.

The minutes dragged by as she fucked him relentlessly then pulled out and stepped back, watching as he rolled onto his side on the table, not wanting to let either his mutilated cock and balls nor his ruptured arsehole rest against anything solid.

"Open that pretty little mouth for me," she told him as she moved to stand by his head, one hand guiding the silicone cock towards his face, the shaft now slick with blood, small grainy peanut size pieces of wet faecal matter and small matted hairs.

He recoiled at the sight and smell, and Zoe snarled and bent, snatching up the hammer that she had violently beaten his testicles with minutes before.

The first blow struck David hard upon the bridge of his nose, shattering the cartilage with ease and almost mashing it flat against his blood features, and she raised the hammer again, swing it down.

His left eye seemed to explode under the impact, liquid and tissue splattering across her sweaty chest, and almost sobbing in excitement, Zoe raised the hammer a third time, concentrating harder now.

The head of the hammer struck David in the centre of his mouth, the force of the blow smashing five teeth from the top row and three from the bottom, the discarded enamel falling back into his throat and being swallowed as David choked against the blood from his gums and his ruptured lips.

She struck him again, this time striking him on the left side of his mouth, the head of the hammer almost sliding past his lips as the teeth came loose.

Nostrils flaring as he fought to breathe through his ruined nose as he began to choke on blood and teeth, David lay virtually helpless as Zoe moved to straddle his face, silicone cock in hand.

With almost zero resistance she pushed it deep into his mouth, bared teeth no longer an obstacle for her. She went deep, waiting until she was certain that the head of the cock was in his throat then pulled it back out, watching as David gagged against the shit and bloody arse hairs coating his lips.

He screamed at her then, finding a measure of courage from some long forgotten well within him, and she lashed out, striking him hard on the left collarbone with the head of the hammer. There was a sickening crack, and the bone, visible through his skin broke, his shoulder seeming to lose its shape.

Intrigued by this new event, she angled the hammer, and struck his right collarbone, this one taking three hard hits before it too suddenly broke.

David screamed, trying to shift himself away from the unbearable pain, his ruined eye a gaping chasm of blood and gore, but the broken ends of the collarbones ground against each other no matter which way he tried to move. Tossing the hammer aside, Zoe reached down with one hand, prodding at his collarbone with her fingers while she touched herself with her free hand, her fingers curling beneath the strap-on that she still wore. "I am so…"

Her words trailed off as the almost deafening thrum of a helicopter suddenly seemed to fill her apartment, and stepping away from her bleeding prisoner, Zoe moved to her balcony and stared out.

From the angle that her apartment was facing, and due to the roofs of the nearby buildings, she was unable to see the majority of Shanklin seafront as it stretched away to the North in the direction of distant Sandown, yet the thrum of the helicopter was loud, as if it were almost on top of where she lived.

As she stood watching, a black helicopter flew noisily into sight from the North, barely thirty feet above the street, a second close behind the first. They continued for a hundred metres, each of them turning as they drew near the end of the street and the Woodland attraction known as Shaklin Chine, the aircraft lowering to the ground. From the vantage point of her balcony, Zoe watched emotionless as figures in orange protective clothing, backpacks and gas masks poured from the open sides of the pair of helicopters, six from each aircraft, all but two of them carrying what appeared to be automatic rifles.

Having delivered their mysterious payload, the helicopters took to the sky almost immediately, and the two small groups of orange-clad figures began to hurry towards down the promenade, weapons raised.

Had they been the victim of chemical warfare?

Was this some form of official attempt to stop the madness that was now erupting in the streets?

In the street below, just as they were about to pass from sight behind the nearby buildings, two of the figures suddenly opened fire on someone out of view, the bursts of gunfire controlled and short.

Then they were hurrying out of sight.

Zoe hesitated a moment long on her balcony, hands unfastening the strap-on to fall to the ground as she stood watching the street for any sight of more of the newcomers yet there were none to see.

Something was happening, something big.

She knew that, yet she felt no desire to find out what it was, nor any hope that this situation could soon be over. She felt nothing whatsoever.

Until she turned and let her gaze settle upon David once again, and the blood rush of excitement coursed up her spine and through her nerve endings.

"Where were we, lover?"

BEN

"Has she gone?"

Ben Grass tensed at the question, then trying his best to stay calm, he turned to study the four teenage girls and one boy standing in the room behind him, being careful not to meet their gaze.

He knew what he would see if he did.

Hatred, dread, disgust, fear.

And why shouldn't they feel those emotions towards him, after all, he had spent the morning trying to murder and rape them.

Oh God, he felt light-headed with shame as the memories of his actions came back in a tsunami of shame and grief, stomach knotting as he recalled the things he had done to their fellow students.

Children that he had been tasked to look after, children that had trusted him.

The day had started so well, with he, and his three fellow teachers from Crookhorn Park Academy setting out from Portsmouth harbour on the ferry to the Isle of Wight. He had driven the minibus while Jean, Abby, and Helena (Miss Tate, Miss Cole, and Mrs Davis to the pupils), had sat in the vehicles rear with the thirteen children, nine girls and four boys, all aged between thirteen and sixteen.

It was the end of the school year, and six weeks of summer fun awaited both pupils and their teachers, filling them all with joy.

They had reached the island with no difficulties, and apart from an awkward situation between McKenzie Johnson and Sally Brooks in the back row of the minibus, discovered by the eagle-eyed Mrs Davis, the drive to Shanklin had been uneventful.

Exchanging knowing looks with Abby, the schools geography teacher, and his lover, Ben had parked the minibus, and they had all filed out into the carpark, several of the kids moaning about how hot the sun was.

"You'll all be moaning when it's cold again!" Jean, biology teacher for the seniors, had teased them all, and they had moaned their agreement, drawing smiles from Ben.

Helena had announced that they would be spending half hour in the arcades along from the cliff-lift, then they would be back in the minibus and heading to the wildlife sanctuary that they had come to visit, and with a cheer, the teens had surged away.

As Jean and Helena had hurried after the group, shouting out for them to stay together and not give the school a bad name, Abby had turned to look at Ben and wiggled her eyebrows suggestively at him. "Hello, Mr Grass."

"Hello, Miss Cole," he had responded, fighting to control himself as a jolt of lust had pulsed through his body. At five feet two inches, she was almost a foot shorter than he, her lean frame dwarfed by his own muscular body, yet in the bedroom she was a tiger.

He had licked at his lips, trying to stay calm as she had turned, the fingers of her right hand casually tracing across the growing bulge in the front of the jeans he wore, and once again her was struck with how much she resembled the actress who had played Missandei in Game of Thrones.

"Well," he had chuckled. "What now?"

"Oh, I don't know," she had sent him a mischievous grin. "I'm sure they will be fine having fun in the arcades, shall we find somewhere quiet?"

Ben had laughed aloud, head shaking and then she had grasped him by the hand, leading him off towards the shops that sat beyond the arcades.

The sudden boom of the explosion had made them both flinch and duck, Ben instinctively wrapping his arms about his lover as they had stared up. High in the sky, black fragments began to fall towards the sea, while a cloud of white smoke, glittering under the intense sun, had begun to drift downwards.

"Who the Hell lets bloody fireworks off in the day?" Abby had laughed, head shaking and frowning, Ben had studied the white cloud as it had drifted down towards the ground.

"Is that what it was?"

"What else?" she had grinned at him.

Nodding, he had let himself be led, coughing as his throat had begun to itch.

"Are you OK?" she had sent him a glance of concern. "Man flu?"

"Whatever," he had grinned back.

Turning past a fish and chip shop, Abby had led him through into an open doorway marked with a sign for toilets, and into a disabled toilet cubicle.

Ben had barely managed to close and lock the door before Abby had been on him, hands dragging his tee shirt up as she had kissed her way up to his muscled chest, her tongue swirling over his abdominal muscles.

He had cursed in excitement, and grinning up at him, Abby had sat down on the lid of the toilet and sat upon it, her hands feverishly trying to open his trouser zipper.

Coughing violently, Ben had watched as she had dragged his jeans and boxer shorts down about his thighs, a shaky sigh escaping her as she had grasped the base of his hard dick in one hand. "Do all P.E teachers have big cocks?"

Feeling dizzy from the coughing, one arm resting against the wall for support, he had stayed silent, watching emotionlessly as she had spread her lips wide and sheathed him with her mouth. He had grunted, the sound coming more from memory than actual enjoyment, watching as she had bobbed her head back and forth, moaning loudly about the meat filling her mouth.

For almost a minute she had worked away at him, lips sliding, mouth pulling, before she had given a grunt of confusion and sat back, brow furrowing as she had looked up at him. "What's the matter?"

She had gasped in shock as he had grasped at her head with his large hands, and turned her about, his right boot kicking out to lift the lid of the toilet. Abby had twisted violently in his strong grip, recoiling as she had stared down into the toilet basin and glancing past her writhing body, he had seen the dark copper water, specked with what looked like blood where the previous occupant hadn't flushed, while a thick streak of almost orange shit ran up the side of the basin like the skid mark of a car tyre.

Pushing downwards, he had steered her head into the basin until her movement had been stopped as she had braced her hands on the rim of the toilet as she shouted at him. "Ben, what the fuck are…"

Her words had turned to a scream as he had kicked at her left arm, the elbow breaking with a sickening crack. As she toppled off-balance, he pushed her down once more, the corner of his mouth twisting into the hint of a smile as he heard her begin to gargle on the bloody urine below as her air ran out. Dragging her back, he spun her in his grasp to see the orange shit was now smeared across her lips and left cheek. She gagged as some slid into her mouth, her gasping chokes as she sucked air back into her lungs turning to a screech of shock and then agony as he pushed his thumbs into her eyes.

Ben had felt the orbs pop beneath the pressure, what felt like jelly oozing past his thumbs, and he had released the screaming woman to slide from the toilet to the tiled floor. Blood had ran down her face from the ruins of her eye sockets as she had thrashed about in pain and fear, the lids opening and closing like mouths whose teeth had been torn free.

From somewhere beyond the closed toilet door, a scream sounded, followed by another, then another, a rising chorus of fear and pain borne of a hundred or more voices.

For almost a minute, Ben had stood staring down at her calmly, knowing full well that he had just blinded the woman that he loved, yet he felt no guilt or shame at all.

With almost complete apathy, he had batted aside the blindly reaching hand of the screaming Abby, then grasped her by her hair, turning her head towards the toilet basin then smashed her face down into the hard porcelain rim three times in quick succession. Bloody teeth had fallen into the dirty water, others skittering away across the tiles, and acting purely on impulse, Ben had turned her back towards him, then hissed in pain as she had suddenly lashed out with a small folding knife that she had dragged from somewhere on her person. Ben had seen it several times before when she had stopped to cut wildflowers on their frequent country hikes.

Realising that it had nearly taken his own eyes, wincing at where the small blade had nicked the bridge of his nose, Ben had disarmed her of the small weapon, then turned the blade and punched it deep into the side of her throat.

Abby had begun to gag, choking on the blood that filled her throat, and casting the blade aside, Ben had bent, and pushed his still hard cock in through the tagged wound. The grip upon his cock had been like glue, reminding him of the time that he had tried to fuck a jar of marmite as a teenager, yet with each thrust the wound widened, the skin splitting as his thick cock gouged ever deeper.

She had died then, the love of his life, blind and bleeding out while he fucked her oesophagus with quick hard thrusts.

Stepping back, bored, Ben had dragged up his underwear and jeans and stepped back out of the disabled toilet room, then moved back to retrieve the blade. Folding it up, Ben had placed it in a front pocket and then strode out into the bright sunshine.

Chaos had ruled in every direction that he had looked in; women and children being raped and killed by men and teenage boys, the horrified looks on the victims faces suggesting that their attackers were friends or family.

Once more he had pictured Abby as he had left her, dead and blind on the floor of the toilet, yet again it sparked no emotion.

He had known that something was wrong with him, with everyone around him, yet he had been an emotional blank slate.

Movement at the corner beside the fish and chip shop had made him turn towards it, watching apathetically as a blonde woman had run past, leading a ginger haired woman by the hand, shouting back at her. "Run E.V!"

The urge to follow the women sparked him into stepping forward as he watched the pair drop down to hide in one of the seafront bus shelters, but then he had turned back to the corner, watching with interest as a familiar figure had staggered around it, one hand clasping to her front as she sobbed aloud.

Helena. Mrs Davis.

She had seen him then, her free hand rising as if to attract his attention but then a large teenage boy, McKenzie Johnson, had rushed quickly around the corner and slammed her violently up against the wall of the fish and chip shop. His interest piqued, Ben had strode towards the struggling pair, hearing the woman grunt in pain as the teenage boy had alternated between punching her in the stomach and the face. Both had turned towards him as he had drawn near, the teeth of the teenage boy bared in a feral snarl, a wild animal not wanting to share its prey, while Helena had met his curious gaze with a pleading look, her voice breaking as she had sobbed.

"Help Ben!"

In reply, he had retrieved the small blade from his front pocket, unfolded it and passed it to the teenager, then stood watching as the boy had laughingly sliced the terrified teachers face to ribbons with quick slashes.

Her cheeks little more than slivers of meat, her tongue now five strips of flesh, and her lips hanging from her face, Helena had tried to call out to Ben again, her words replaced by a bubbling, agonized lowing like a cow being slaughtered.

Ben had walked calmly away.

The following couple of hours had been a blur of violence as Ben had found himself going after the female students and Jean, Miss Tate, chasing them all around Shanklin seafront, aided by a now blood-covered and feral McKenzie Johnson.

Together they had managed to kill two of the younger three boys who unlike almost every other male, were not attacking anyone, Ben choking the life from one as he had sodomised him violently with a broken bottle, while the now maniacal McKenzie had disembowelled the other with a meat cleaver he had taken from a beach side restaurant.

Then they had gone after the girls.

Throughout it all, Ben had felt nothing, nothing but an urge to punish the dumb, mewling little cunts that had made his job so hard with their constant whining and bitching.

Throughout it all, Jean, had fought to keep the girls safe from harm, the expression of grief and heartbreak upon her features each time that he and McKenzie had managed to capture and kill one of the little bitches like an injection of adrenaline into his core.

And mutilate and kill them they had.

First up had been Sally Brooks, the pair catching her as the group had tried to get back inside the school minibus, only for he and McKenzie to rush the group from an alleyway.

They had fled, rushing towards the beach, and for a moment Ben had nearly given chase, then turned back to watch as McKenzie had stripped the clothes from the teenager that he had been flirting with earlier.

Ben had let his gaze drift over the sixteen-year-olds naked form with the same apathy he had watched his beloved Abby die.

His beloved Abby.

So why had he felt nothing?

Ben had never liked Sally despite her model looks and figure, finding her devoid of personality and intelligence while his fellow male teachers had made crude jokes to each other about the girl, nudging and winking.

Whistling to himself, he had unfastened the door and turned on the ignition. Walking back around the van, he had paused, watching as he saw McKenzie push himself violently into the screaming girls arse, hands grasping at her large breasts as he began to thrust away at her. Turning away, Ben had open the bonnet of the minibus and put the arm up to keep it open, then instructed the boy to bring the girl over to where he had waited.

For a moment it had seemed that he would not obey but then with a grin, he had done as asked, pulling free of the girl before rising and dragging her towards the minibus.

To her credit, she had fought like a thing possessed as the boy had bent her forward and pushed back inside her, then Ben had thrown her trailing long blonde hair into the engine where it had gotten itself caught up in the fan belt. She had screeched in agony as most of the hair in the centre of her head had been ripped free in one go, the raw power of the engine degloving her scalp with ease.

McKenzie had whooped with delight, and Ben had frowned as he had studied the screaming girl with long hair either side of her head and the centre bald. "You look like you are raping Terry Nutkins!"

McKenzie had glanced at him with a look of confusion, not understanding the reference, and Ben had turned and stared off towards the beach, not wanting to let the others get too far away from them.

The boy had ignored him, hands reaching beneath the screaming Sally to maul at her lurching breasts, and turning away, Ben had walked to the rear of the minibus, opened it, and removed the jack from inside. Returning to the front of the minibus, he had slid it under the vehicle, and pumped up and down with the handle, watching as the front offside of the minibus had started to slowly rise upwards.

McKenzie had appeared beside him, dragging the girl with him, the whites of her eyes wide and insane as she stared out from the mask of blood on her face.

"What are you…" the boy had begun only for Ben to grasp at the girl and throw her heavily to the ground. Grasping at her hands, he had pivoted his hips and swung, watching as the naked girl had slid screaming across the gravel of the car park, her body sliding under the raised tyre. Then he had thrust out an arm and turned the long handle, releasing the jack, and dragging it out from underneath the vehicle.

The minibus had dropped, the tyre dropping down to rest upon the girls chest with a sickening crunch as her sternum and several ribs cracked. Beneath the weight of the minibus, Sally had wheezed a gasping blood-flecked breath, hands uselessly pushing at the tyre, while beneath the vehicle her feet had kicked a staccato drumbeat as she spasmed in agony.

As he had stood watching, the tyre had suddenly dropped an inch or two as more of the girls bones had given out, a geyser of blood erupting from her open mouth, and curious, Ben had stepped closer and stared down into her wide eyes. Once again he knew that he should be feeling something.

But he had been a blank slate.

Or he had been until he had pictured torturing and killing his students once again.

He had blinked as liquid had suddenly begun to splash down onto the dying girl and had half-turned to find the boy at his side now pissing onto

Sally's bloody face, the teenagers mouth split in a broad grin as he did so.

Ben had turned back to the now dead girl, watching as the stream of hot piss began to move slowly across her face, cleaning the blood away from her features as McKenzie aimed carefully like a man pissing shit off the sides of a toilet bowl.

Then, not waiting to see if McKenzie was following him Ben had turned away and begun to run towards the beach where the others had fled.

"Mr Grass?"

"Don't talk to him, he's a monster" the hissed reply came from a second voice, barely loud enough for him to hear yet the tone of the voice snatched him from his memories.

Heaving a shaky breath that seemed to rattle from his lungs, Ben turned to study the five teenagers that were stood huddled against the far wall of the shop in which they were hiding. His eyes dropped to the screwdriver that the foremost of them, a lean girl of thirteen named Chloe, was holding before her and realised that it was she that had just spoken.

"You don't need that…" he nodded towards the makeshift weapon. "I am not going to hurt you. I promise."

"Like you didn't hurt Jez and Anthony, or Julia and Sally, or Rebecca and Cat?" Chloe asked bitterly, her elfin features twisting. "Oh wait, you did hurt them didn't you…you hurt them, you tortured them, and you killed them…didn't you!"

The last two words were shouted, and Ben felt his legs almost give way as memories of what he had done returned to him once more, his breath coming in ragged gasps as he relived the horror of his actions.

They had caught up with Julia Harris shortly after reaching the beach and found her trying to hide behind a wooden breakwater. As the others had screamed in terror and backed away from where they had been waiting some distance from the lone girl, Ben and McKenzie had dragged the fifteen-year-old from her hiding place. She had fought like a demon, her fear giving her a strength that had surprised them both, and somehow the girl had almost broke free from their grasp.

She had stopped struggling though when Ben had grasped at her trailing hair with one hand, stopping her as she had tried to flee then snatched the meat cleaver from his teenage accomplice and chopped her hard in the lower back. The blade had bitten in deep, causing the girl to jerk and scream, and Ben had wrenched the cleaver free and chopped hard into her spine once more, aiming for the lumber region. Her legs had folded beneath her, and she had hit the wet sand face first, blood blossoming out through the back of her grey tee shirt.

Screams of denial had snatched Ben's attention from the incapacitated girl to find the others standing staring at them in horror, only for the group to run as McKenzie had given chase, roaring at them in excitement.

Dropping down to kneel on the wet sand beside the screaming girl, Ben had dragged her tee shirt up to study the wounds in her back. Just above the girls waist were the two horizontal cuts, each roughly seven inches in length, the pair angled above each other like a lopsided equals mathematical sign.

Holding her down with a hand upon the back of her head, Ben had dropped the cleaver and reached down with his free hand to press above the wounds. Blood had welled as they gaped wide, and on impulse he had pushed the fingers into the lowest wound, probing until he was up to his second knuckle. The broken edges of spine had rubbed against his exploring digits where he had severed her spine, and without giving it too much thought, he had retrieved the cleaver and used the blade to slice the ends of the wounds longer.

The girl had writhed in agony as he had pushed his entire right hand into her body through the wound, fingers searching from what he knew of human biology, then with a grunt, he fastened his grip about the object he had found. His expression blank, he had begun to drag it back out through the hole he had made, cutting with the cleaver when muscles and tissue stopped his crude surgery.

Sitting back on his heels, he had raised the girls left kidney before his face, fingers turning it as he studied it intently, deep red in colour and warm on his palm. Without giving it any thought, he raised it to his mouth and bit deeply, taking off a good chunk.

The meat had been surprisingly firm to the bite, yet as Ben had worked it with his teeth, blood and fluids had flowed from it into his mouth, making eating it easier.

The girl had screamed, and he had turned his gaze to find her staring back at him, eyes wide in terror as she had watched him eat her kidney. He had chewed calmly as he had held her gaze, then taken another bite before casting the remaining chunk away to the wet sand to be snatched up by a seagull.

Chewing on the gristly meat in his mouth, Ben had turned to study the girl's face as she rested her head on the wet sand, her agonised vocalisations having finally fallen silent as her teenage body went into shock.

"Julia Harris," he had muttered her name about the half-chewed kidney. "You never pulled your weight in my P.E class. Always lying to me that you can't run."

He had picked the meat cleaver back up as he had talked, his voice calm and measured, even as he had raised the weapon and hacked off first one of the teenage girls feet and then the other, the second taking three hard chops.

As blood had poured from the stumps of her legs, the tide had rolled in about them then washed out once more, taking one of the feet with it. Ben had watched it vanish into the waves then turned back to Julia. "Now I believe you can't run."

She had not replied, blood loss and shock having sent her into unconsciousness and Ben had raised the bloody fingers of his free hand to poke at a bit of raw kidney that had gotten stuck between two of his teeth.

He gagged at the memory of what he had done, his throat tightening and saliva filling his mouth as he leaned forwards and vomited violently upon the floor of the room.

The five children watched him in silence, only a grunt of disgust escaping one of their number as a second wave of vomit escaped him, rushing up, swelling his throat, and then pouring from his open mouthp to splatter noisily upon the floor. The smell hit him almost at once, sour, and hot, and he staggered back, a hand covered in dried blood rising to try and clear the clinging vomit from his mouth and nostrils as he blinked to clear the dancing lights from his vision.

Abruptly a cacophony of banging erupted on the door behind him, and fighting the waves of nausea and stomach cramps, Ben forced himself to turn and face it.

"Oh my God, she's gonna kill us!" the remaining male of the group almost sobbed from the back of the room, and Ben winced, knowing the gentle boy was probably right.

The banging ceased without warning then returned, more insistent than before and Ben bowed his head as he pictured the person on the other side, his head shaking in denial.

Jean. Miss Tate.

Just over half hour ago it had been she within the room, desperately trying to keep he and McKenzie out, while they in turn had fought to get through the door to kill them all.

Then his vision had cleared, and the burning scratchy sensation in his throat had gone, leaving him with the crushing guilt and horror of what he had done that morning.

By the time that he had finally left the beach and the remains of Julia, then headed after McKenzie and the others, the entire front of the promenade had turned to chaos.

Murder and rape had been taking place everywhere he had turned, while at the end of the seafront near where the road angled to head up the steep hill, a minibus had been set ablaze while men had stood about watching the conflagration with blank expressions while its occupants screamed on pain and terror.

Once again, he had questioned his own lack of empathy, knowing that the things he had done, the things that others were doing, were wrong on every level.

Yet he felt no guilt of shame with that knowledge. In fact, it had only been when he had pictured capturing and killing the other children and his last fellow faculty member that he had felt any spark of emotion at all.

Like a shell of a man, he had walked down the promenade, stepping past the burned remains of a dog, his head turning back and forth as he had searched for his prey. Several of the men and older male youths running amok had glanced his way, seen the blood upon his body and the meat cleaver in his hand and continued, perhaps caught up in their own personal hunts to feel something.

To feel anything.

Striding onwards, he had turned his head, watching the countless scenes of madness that were erupting around him with boredom, knowing that he should be disgusted but feeling nothing but apathy.

With a mind-numbing screech, a heavily pregnant woman, wealthy by her clothing, had burst from an alleyway, almost colliding with Ben only to pivot aside as she had seen him. Off balance, she had ran into a lamppost and bounced back, one hand clasped to her bleeding face, another to her bulging stomach as she had fallen, the back of her head bouncing hard from the pavement.

Ben had watched with disinterest as she had struggled to rise, then screamed in terror as two men had lurched from the alleyway from which she had fled.

Shrieking in excitement, the pair, Turkish or Arabic of descent and wearing aprons stained with all manner of liquids, leaped upon the screaming pregnant woman, pinning her down as she had fought to rise and run. Leaning against the wall, Ben had picked a bag of popcorn from the display hanging in the doorway of the gift shop he had stopped beside and opened it, shovelling a handful into his mouth as he had watched the scene before him with growing boredom. With a chuckle, the younger of the men had drawn a meat cleaver from his apron, and knelt beside the squirming woman, while the other had torn her clothing up to expose her swollen stomach, a hysterical laugh escaping him as he had squirmed his tongue over her bump.

As Ben had stood watching, the first man had placed the cleaver against the woman's stomach and raised it high, then chopped down several times hard.

The woman had screamed in agony, her legs bucking, and as blood had sprayed across the men, the hands of the older man had pushed excitedly in through the horrific gash his friend had just made.

Ben had raised an eyebrow as the man had suddenly dragged a baby from within the cavity of the woman's stomach, its bloody body pale, the cord connecting it to its dying mother blue and glistening.

The infant had cried at its untimely removal, eyes scrunched tight against the blistering sunlight overhead, and then fallen silent as the younger man had dropped the cleaver and twisted the baby's head, wringing its neck in the way one might kill a chicken.

Even as it had died, the older man had pulled a metal bar from the floor beside him, previously unseen by Ben, then proceeded to shove it up between the legs of the child, skewering it as the metal punched out through the top of its tiny skull.

With a roar of triumph, the man had raised his grisly trophy high, then both men had been off once more, rushing back into the alleyway, the younger man shouting to someone to light the grill.

Ben had watched them go, knowing their intent but feeling no disgust or horror at their actions, nor shame at not having intervened.

Sighing, he had begun to walk once more, calmly emptying the remains of the popcorn bag into the gory cavity of the dead woman's stomach. As he had reached the far end of the amusement arcade, he had suddenly heard the unmistakable thup-thup-thup of a helicopter and turned to watch as one had begun to lower over the seafront. For a moment, it had swayed in place, then without warning it had crashed, the top rotor whipping across the seafront before it had exploded into a fireball.

For long moments he had studied it in silence, while all around him killers and victims had run amok, caught up in their own agendas. All save for a man stood before the ice-cream shop staring back towards the inferno, a huge black dog by his side.

His curiosity flared then faded, and Ben turned away, continuing down the long road.

He had caught up with McKenzie at the entrance to the Shaklin Chine tourist attraction, a wooded coastal ravine filled with walkways, fibreglass dinosaurs and colourful lights.

As he had jogged up to the gates, he had found the teenage boy smashing the face of a naked teenage girl onto the edge of an old stone wall, the wet sounds that each impact made revealing that she was long dead.

It had been Rebecca Marsh, a member of his running team and a child that he had always found to be personable and intelligent. Yet as he watched McKenzie grip the corpse of the small, lean girl by the ankles and swing it violently over the wall into the void below, Ben felt nothing but boredom, his emotions replaced by an almost dreamlike languor.

Not even bothering to see where the girl had landed on the beach below, Ben had strode up through the gates, and past the small wooden ticket booth. He turned as he drew level with it, watching as man within it strangled a younger woman with blonde dreadlocks, the pair wearing the same uniform. Striding onwards, he had scanned the tree-lined walkways and paths that he could see intently for any sign of his prey, then turned to watch as McKenzie raced past him towards the old house that sat some distance ahead of them, the signs upon its face declaring that it was the heritage centre.

A face had peered out through one of the small square panes of glass in a doorway, and Ben had broken into a run as he had recognised one of the remaining students.

What had followed had been carnage as he and McKenzie had broken down the outer door of the building and forced their way inside. Three uniformed women had tried to rush at he and the boy as they had gained entry, makeshift weapons in hand, yet they had all been on the verge of being classed as elderly and he had dispatched them to lie dying on the floor of the first room, bodies rent wide with wounds from his meat cleaver.

"Catherine!" the shrill, pained voice of Jean had torn through the room, and he had turned to find her stood in an adjoining corridor, the remaining children behind her, each screaming in denial as they watched McKenzie dragging another girl backwards.

Excitement flaring, Ben had stepped towards the group only for them to turn and run, abandoning the girl to her fate, as they had slammed a wooden door behind them, followed by the loud click of several locks.

"Don't hurt me!" the girl had screamed as McKenzie had dragged her violently into the centre of the room, her hands raised before her body, pleading. "Please don't hurt me Mr Grass…don't please…don't hurt me!"

He had taken the fingers of her left hand with one sweep of the cleaver, and as her digits had taken flight, she had screamed falsetto as blood had poured from the stumps.

McKenzie had released her, and she had stumbled away, tripping and falling over the body of an old woman whose throat Ben had opened with his meat cleaver, and he had stepped over the girl, studying her face as she sobbed and pleaded, a chunk of snot hanging from her right nostril like a bungee jumper.

Movement beside Ben had made him turn, watching as the teenage boy had reappeared holding what had looked like an oar save for the fact that the paddle was metal.

With sweep of his arm the boy had dropped the metal end down onto the rotund stomach of the girl, the weight of the item sending it slicing through her clothes and skin.

Blood had gushed from the terrible wound as her tightly packed intestines had bulged their way either side of what Ben had realised was an old head-spade, designed for killing whales and no doubt part of an exhibition there.

The girl had wailed piteously, and the teenage boy had raised the blade on the end of the long wooden pole once more, then brought it crashing down hard onto her head.

Instead of being split in two, the skull of the girl came apart under the impact; brains, blood and bone seeming to explode over the polished wooden floor about her.

Almost at once Ben had strode down the corridor towards the locked wooden door, striking it with the meat cleaver as he tried to force his way in, while McKenzie stabbed at its surface with pokes of the bloody head-spade.

Time had lost all meaning to him as he had stood there, hacking violently at the door, excitement flaring within him each time he had heard a sob or scream from behind it, until suddenly the door had opened wide.

Off balance, he had stumbled forward into the room, the cleaver imbedded in the door. He had landed hard, cursing as he had tried to rise to his feet, emotions spiking as he had seen the scared faces of those before him.

With a roar, McKenzie had tried to charge into the room only for Jean to rush forward and snatch the meat cleaver from the door, a wild swing from it almost decapitating the naked teenager as he had roared at her, the blade opening the boys throat.

A chair had struck Ben over the back, and he had fallen to his side, glaring up at Jean as she had stood beyond the door, leaning heavily against it as she had coughed violently.

He had pushed himself to his hands and knees, staring up at the four girls and one boy, his lips cracking into a snarl only for him to suddenly blink in shock, tears filling his eyes as the realisation of what he had done assailed him with the force of a hurricane, the sudden return of his emotions nearly laying him to the ground; guilt, shame, regret.

All of them were running wild within him now, turning his soul black with grief.

"Jean…?" he had managed to gasp, his eyes rising to where she had been stood in the doorway, and she had half turned towards them, her now blood covered features twisted into a sneer as she had let her gaze drift from him to the children huddled against the wall, then back again, her nose wrinkling in disgust as she had snarled at them.

"I'm going to kill you all!"

"I did the things you said!" Ben forced himself from his memories, trying to not recall the terror he had felt as he had rushed at the door and slammed it, locking the now raging Jean outside of the room. Turning, he forced himself to meet the accusing gaze of the five young teenagers, his voice breaking as he spoke. "As soon as this is all over I am going to hand myself over to the authorities. I promise you all. I have to. I have to pay for what I have done. But right now, I am going to do my best to keep you all alive."

There was a heavy silence as they stared back at him, fear, and distrust in their eyes, and then Chloe spoke. "How?"

Ben winced, fighting the dread in his stomach as the assault upon the door began once more. "I don't know."

ZOE

"Hey, are you still with me?"

On the blood covered table before her, David stared up at her with his huge lidless remaining eye. For a moment, she wasn't sure if he was conscious or not, then his mouth moved silently, the raw flesh where she had cut his lips free glistening with blood, revealing his bloody gums and one remaining tooth.

Humming to herself, Zoe turned to study the small pile of body parts that she had sourced from her prisoner, her eyes travelling over the bloody lips, curled like slugs as they sat beside his nipples, both of his ears and his eyelids, each slick with blood.

Returning her gaze to his face, Zoe shuddered as she studied the ragged triangular hole above his mouth where his nose had once been, blood bubbling at the wound as he gave a shaky breath. Smiling, Zoe lowered her gaze to her bloody hands, studying the metal cutters that she used for her art in her left, before shifting her gaze to her right palm. The bloody hunk of skin and cartilage that sat there in no way resembled a nose, save perhaps for the two nostrils, still filled with coarse grey hairs.

She curled her fingers back, making a soft honk-honk noise as she held his one-eyed gaze, and he moaned back at her, a wounded animal gone mad.

Placing the nose down on the small pile of body parts, she let her eyes drift over him, brow furrowing. "What can we do next? Ah, I know…"

Somehow he stayed silent, but his bloody mutilated body shook violently as she stepped close beside him, her eyes fixed to his bound hands.

"Shall we take your fingernails off?"

He moaned, a large bloody bubble forming and then popping as he started to panic, drawing a chuckle from Zoe. "No, I'll leave your fingernails, it's so unoriginal isn't it. Let's try this instead."

She had barely finished speaking before she pushed the metal cutters between the thumb and finger next to it on his right hand, catching the fleshy webbing between them in its jaws. David tensed, arm pulling back on the bonds, but he was bound tight. Releasing a shaky breath, Zoe licked at her lips, and squeezed the rubber handles of the cutters together, a moan of pleasure escaping her as the blades, sharp enough to cut through metal, sliced through the meaty fold as if she were cutting fresh chicken.

David went insane against his bonds, his tormented screams intensifying as his frantic movements forced his broken collar bones to grind. Blood welled from the deep slice between his thumb and index finger, the wound a tiny mouth that gaped wide, and excited once more, Zoe moved to the webbing between the index finger and middle finger, cutting once more. There was less webbing here, and thus less blood issued forth from the wound, turning Zoe's enjoyment to anger. With a grim face, she continued along his hand, cutting webbing as she went, then moved to the other, only smiling again as she cut deep into the fleshy fold beside his thumb and the bleeding matched the first wound.

Heaving a contented sigh, she glanced up at David as he lay there, teeth gritted together as his single eye stared up at the ceiling overhead, the sight of that one remaining tooth seeming to mock her.

"No," she shook her head as she moved to stand nearer his head, brow furrowing as she studied the lone tooth with irritation. "That won't do at all."

Reaching down with the metal cutters, she fastened them to the tooth, holding his head still with her other hand as she squeezed on the handles. There was the briefest of resistance and then the tooth sheared in half at an angle, exposing the nerve.

In agony, David hissed in a sharp breath, then screamed as the air touched the nerve, his entire body seeming to shake as he thrashed wildly about.

"What to do," she frowned as she studied him once more, a finger rising to tap at her lips as her haze drifted back down to his large cock, freshly skinned, shiny from where it still bled and wept.
 Crouching, she let her gaze drift over the few remaining items on her tray, and then nodded, rising confidently to place several of them upon the table.

"First things first," she reached out with her left hand, fastening her fingers about the slimy meat of his cock, still surprisingly girthy despite the wounds that she had inflicted upon it earlier. Raising her left hand, she placed the small plastic funnel over it, her nose wrinkling in irritation as she tried unsuccessfully to fit the bottom end into his urethra. Frowning, she placed the funnel down then retrieved the metal cutters once more, and casually cut into each side of his urethra, extending the slit, then pushed the funnel into the new larger opening.

On the table, David lay still, unmoving despite the horrors that she was perpetrating against his body, and Zoe cursed softly, forcing herself to concentrate as she retrieved a small canister of lighter fluid and poured it in the funnel, watching as the flammable liquid washed through into his cock. Somehow, against the odds, David still didn't react, and Zoe tensed, fearing for a moment that she had killed him and that their time together was over but then she saw the faint rise and fall of his chest.

She studied him breathing for a moment, one hand still clasping to his floppy, blood smeared cock with the plastic funnel poking from the end. Then she turned back to the task at hand and picked up her lighter, thumbing the flame into life as she dropped it into the large open end of the funnel.

There was a second of stillness then a gout of fire shot upwards from his urethra like a fat snake breathing flames, a blood-stained cock-dragon belching fury into the sky like a geyser of lava piss.

David awoke then, seemingly oblivious to his broken collar bones as he strained against his bonds, his one eye staring down at his cock as it spat fire.

Zoe giggled as the memory of an old Eddie Murphy gag about gonorrhea returned to her from his stand-up days; *The doctor told me I might feel a slight burning sensation when I urinate. Burning sensation? Fire come out of my dick! I can't pee indoors, I'd burn the Goddamn house down!*

There was a sudden crash from the front of her home, and snarling, Zoe spun towards the noise, hands rising before her defensively as three orange figures suddenly rushed into her living room.

"Put your fucking hands up!" one of them screamed as it took quick steps towards her, the automatic rifle that it was carrying pointing her way, while the other two spread out behind the first.

Zoe did as instructed, her face impassive as she stared back at the three figures in her home, taking in their orange protective suits, akin to the overalls that her father had worn as a paint sprayer. Each of the three was wearing some form of gas mask, though only one of the others was also carrying a weapon, an automatic rifle like the first.

"Jenkins!" the unarmed figure, a woman by its voice and the long black hair that was tied back from its head stated. "Don't shoot. Just keep her there."

"Fuck!" the man before her gave a shake of his head. "Look at what she's done to this guy!"

"Do not shoot her!" the woman repeated, then cocked her head towards the other figure as it stood watching. "Watson, cut her prisoner free!"

"He's mine!" Zoe warned, freezing the man in place just as he had started to move towards where David was tied, his rifle rising to point over at her.

"Listen!" the woman stepped forward a pace, her open hands rising before her in a placating manner as she continued. "We know that this isn't your fault…we just need to take you into custody so we can talk to you…let us help you…"

"Don't!" Zoe warned the man as he took a tentative step forward, surprised at the anger she suddenly felt when faced with losing David, the focal point of the only emotion that she had experienced since the change had taken her. "I'm warning you!"

"Fuck this!" Jenkins snarled. "I'm shooting!"

"Stand down!" the woman shouted. "We need her, she is one of the only live infected we have!"

"Infected," Zoe repeated her words, her gaze drifting to settle upon the woman, her brow creasing.

With a grunt, the man Jenkins moved quickly, dropping his weapon as he grappled Zoe, pinning her arms to her sides with his superior strength, while the other man, Watson, hurried to David's side.

"Have you got her?" the woman seemed unsure, and snarling, one arm wrapping tight about

Zoe's throat, while his other pinned her wrists behind her, Jenkins gave a grunt of confirmation.

"Aye, but we should have shot her, Kent."

"Dr Kent," the woman corrected him, her eyes bright above the gas mask as she stepped closer to him and Zoe, studying her intently before glancing past them both. "Watson how is he?"

"I'm amazed he's alive," the reply came, clear disbelief in the voice. "Shit, the things she's done to him; multiple lacerations, penile destruction, removal of teeth, nipples, lips, ears, nose and eyelids, possible sodomy. It'd be kinder if he didn't make it, doc!"

"Just untie him," she snapped, her gaze returning to Zoe as she squirmed within the grip of the stronger Jenkins. "Why did you do this?"

"You tell me," Zoe found herself replying, her eyes boring into those of the woman. "Who are you, what is this all about?"

"All in good time," Doctor Kent told her, the gaze of the woman shifting as the bloodied figure of David moved into view, helped by the man, Watson.

Zoe turned her head as best as she was able, her teeth baring in a feral snarl as she realised that they were taking him from her, taking him away and she hadn't finished yet. They were ruining everything.

David had half-turned his face towards her as she snarled, a strangled, raw choking sob of terror erupting from his throat and ruined mouth as he saw her staring back at him. With what seemed to be superhuman effort considering his injuries, David pushed Watson violently away from him, the man crying out as his legs hit the coffee table and he fell over it. For a fraction of a second Jenkins released the pressure on Zoe as he turned to watch his colleague fall, and a second was more than enough.

With an animal snarl, she dragged the arm about her throat up and sank her teeth into it, finding a wedge of flesh even through the protective suit. The man screamed in agony, and she span in his arms, hands dragging up his gas mask, obscuring his vision. Even as he took a faltering step back, she was bending and snatching up his rifle, reversing it before sending the butt hammering hard at his head.

Doctor Kent screamed, half turning to run only to stumble and fall as Zoe swung the rifle, cracking the woman in the back of the skull with it.

Even before she had hit the floor along with Jenkins, her eyes rolling in her head, Zoe had rounded the table and struck the other man as he tried to rise, throwing him to the carpet unconscious.

Only then did she turn back to David, eager to get him under her control once more, her body heaving with the excitement of a passion rekindled.

Yet he was nowhere to be found.

David was gone.

BEN

"Are you all ready?" Ben turned to stare back at the five young teenagers opposite, seeing the fear in their eyes. They still weren't sure of him.

In truth he didn't blame them at all.

He had been a monster.

And how was he to know that he wouldn't become one once again, flipping as easily as Jean had moments after he had crashed into the room.

She was now behaving just as he had.

But why? What the Hell was going on?

And why hadn't the teenagers behind him, and those he had killed, changed like McKenzie had?

He winced as he considered the teenager, feeling regret as he recalled the boys violent death, his head nearly cut from his shoulders.

Yes, McKenzie had brutally raped and killed his fellow students, and Mrs Davis, but he had been under the same influence as Ben had.

It wasn't their fault.

Yet they had done the actions with their own hands. They had purposely sought out their victims.

If the blame wasn't theirs then whose was it?

Swallowing the tightness in his throat, Ben cast another glance at the five children he had sworn to protect. "When I tackle her, I want you to run! Whatever you do, don't wait for me"

"We won't!" the short-haired Chloe replied, her features set with a grimace making her look older than her thirteen years, but the others; Jessie, Ruth, Lisa, and Ian seemed less confident than her.

They were all in the same year as Chloe, making them either thirteen or almost so, and he frowned, wondering suddenly if their age had played some part in them not turning feral like the others.

Forcing the thoughts aside, Ben took a step closer to the door, his right hand reaching out towards the handle, his heart hammering in his chest.

"Don't!" the boy, Ian, almost sobbed, his voice breaking as he spoke, and Ben winced, raising a finger to his lips, signalling for him to be silent.

Beyond the door, the hammering began again, more insistent now, and Ben took another deep breath as he considered the plan that he had devised.

On paper it was simple. He would wait until she was attacking the door then open it wide, making her topple off balance just as they had done to him.

Then the children, stood in a line on the wall beside the door, would run out while he slowed her down.

Another chorus of banging erupted on the door before them, seeming to shake it on its hinges and Ben took what he hoped was a steadying breath, telling himself once again that it was just his friend Jean Tate that was trying to get into the room.

He was six feet two inches in height and extremely fit and strong, while Jean stood no higher than five foot four, her frame lean if not muscled.

There was no way that she could beat him in a fight, yet she had the meat cleaver that she had killed McKenzie with, and she was now filled with the same desire to kill and maim that he had been.

Added to which she had the long head-spade that McKenzie had murdered the girl Catherine.

Yet still, the odds were in his favour, surely?

Jen had gone quiet once more, and he gritted his teeth, fastening his hand to the handle, waiting for the assault upon the door to begin once more.

He tensed as he heard movement on the other side of the door, his heart seeming to beat in his chest like a wild animal attempting to escape a trap.

The hammering began once more.

With a silent curse, Ben turned the door handle and stepped to the side as he dragged it open, watching as a figure tumbled forward into the room.

With another curse, he stepped between them and the door, hope taking flight within him as he saw the children flee the room in his peripheral vison.

That hope died the moment he saw the young woman on her knees before him, her long blonde dreadlocks hanging about her face as she turned to look back at him, a bloody knife in her left hand.

Time seemed to slow as he saw the uniform she was wearing, recognition touching him as he realised she was the woman that had been being strangled in the ticket booth near the entrance.

But if she was here? Where was Jean?

Behind him someone screamed, the sound torn from their very soul, and heart in his mouth, Ben span about to find his fellow teacher hacking her meat cleaver back and forth into the throat of

Ruth, her fingers wrapped in the young girls long red hair.

Ben roared in anger and denial, legs bunching as he prepared to rush at his friend, desperate to save the poor girl though it was clear she was dying as she jerked in Jeans grip, blood pouring from her wounds.

The scuff of movement behind him, made Ben tense as he remembered the dreadlocked woman, his body twisting to as he felt rather than saw her rushing him. He cried out as pain lanced through his left hip, then grunted as she collided with him, driving him back to collide with the wall hard.

Her breath filled his lungs as she struggled with him, hot and sour, and acting more from instinct than thought, Ben brought his forehead down quickly, smashing her hard in the face. She screeched and staggered back, her nose mashed flat across her face, her top lip bleeding, and with a roar he rushed at her, his right arm swing in a punch. It struck her hard in the left cheek, almost lifting her from her feet, her arms flailing limply beside her.

Not waiting to see more, Ben turned back towards Jean, crying out as pain lanced into his side once more and with wide eyes he stared down at the knife that was half embedded into his left hip. With a strangled choke of pain, he wrapped his fingers about the blade and dragged it free, blood running over his fingers, and then raised it over his shoulder.

Before him, Ruth was on her back, her right arm detached at the elbow, her face little more than mincemeat as Jean hacked and slashed at the dead girl with the cleaver, her features split with a smile.

Chloe and the others were gone, having taken the chance to escape while they could and Ben forced a grim smile, hoping they would be OK.

Good for them.

Roaring in grief, Ben charged at Jean, cursed as pain lanced through his hip and stumbled, falling to his face as he passed through the open doorway, the knife sliding from his fingers across the floor.

Howling with excitement, Jean leaped past the body of the girl that she had so gleefully butchered, her bloody meat cleaver raised high as she bent down towards Ben, and he cried out, ashamed of his terror.

Above him, Jean suddenly grunted in shock and pain, the cleaver falling from her fingers to the ground beside his head and Ben gagged as hot blood cascaded over him, filling his mouth and nostrils.

Eyes wide, he rolled to the side, watching as Jean staggered away, one hand clasped to the handle of the knife that Ben had only just dropped, the knife that Chloe had buried into the teachers throat.

Suddenly the other children were there; Jessie, Ian, and Lisa, all trying to help him to his feet, while Chloe stood nearby, watching as Jean dropped to her knees. With a choking snarl, the teacher dragged the knife from her throat, a torrent of blood exiting the wound as the blade came free, soaking her clothes.

She tried to stand, the blade pointing towards Chloe, then collapsed to her face in a growing pool of blood, her right foot twitching as she bled out.

"Thank you!" Ben found his voice as he rose, nodding at each of the children then turned to look over at Chloe as she glanced at him. "Thank you!"

The girl was pale, her features drawn as she glanced down at the body of Jean, Miss Tate, then back at him. "She spent all morning trying to save us from you…and now I've just killed her to save you. Make that make sense."

He blinked, overcome with emotion, his head shaking. "I can't…I'm sorry. I'm so sorry."

Chloe sighed bitterly. "We should go."

He nodded, tears in his eyes. "We should."

Gritting his teeth against the pain in his hip and the sticking blood-soaked material of his trousers, Ben let himself be led from the building by the children.

Before leaving the visitor centre, Ben had checked upon the woman with the blonde dreadlocks and found her unconscious, her face beginning to bruise where he had struck her. He had been unsure what to do with her, until Jessie had appeared with some thin rope that she had found in another room, allowing them to bind her hands and feet securely.

Chloe led the way, the knife that she had killed Jean with clasped tight in one hand while Ben carried the meat cleaver, hoping against hope that they wouldn't find a need to use it.

"Fucking Hell!" the lean girl muttered as she reached the entrance to Shanklin Chine, the small group framed by the Victorian iron-wrought gates as they stared along the seafront as they joined her.

"What the fuck is going on?" it was Ben's turn to swear as he studied the scene ahead of them, his brow furrowing in confusion as he saw that two helicopters landed in the road before the arcades.

"Sir?" Ian turned to glance up at him, the voice of the boy filled with hope. "Is it the police?"

Ben stayed silent, watching as a large group of figures in what looked like orange protective clothing began to hurry towards the helicopters, a small group of civilian men and children among them. They split up as they reached the aircraft, several of the orange figures directing the men and the children to separate helicopters. Almost half of them had boarded before a cacophony of screaming suddenly arose and the orange clad figures turned, dropping into crouches as they raised guns before them.

A horde of naked figures seemed to erupt from the arcades like pus pouring from a wound, all of them rushing at the helicopters, each of whom now had their rotor turning overhead, the noise loud.

The new group were women, even from where they were stood watching in shock, Ben could see that, each of them appearing armed with some form of makeshift weapon or another.

There was a sudden burst of gunfire from the crouched figures making Ben flinch in shock, his arms rising before the four remaining children as if they were in danger of being struck by bullets.

The front ranks of the crowd were thrown back as the bullets struck them, the orange figures firing at first in tight concentrated bursts but then all at once as the remaining women drew ever nearer.

Then suddenly they had reached the aircraft, countless women leaping aboard while others threw themselves at the gunmen, weapons hacking wildly.

Heart in his mouth, Ben watched as one of the helicopters suddenly lurched into the air and banked to the right, the children about him gasping in shock and horror as bodies fell from the doorway to the road below, and then the sea as it headed out over the water. For a moment, it looked like the aircraft might make it, that the pilot had managed to evacuate at just the right time, but then without warning the helicopter seemed to fly nose first into the sea, the aircraft coming to pieces with the impact.

"Look!" Lisa pointed with an arm, and Ben cast the short girl a glance and then followed the gesture, his breath catching in his throat as he watched several of the orange clad figures being dragged away from the helicopter by the horde of screaming woman while others continued to butcher their victims beside the aircraft.

"What do we do?" Ian asked, the boy sounding as if he were on the verge of tears and not meeting his gaze, Ben nodded towards the car park which sat halfway between them and the helicopter.

"The school minibus, I have the keys still."

"We can't go down there," Jessie shook her head, her eyes wide behind her glasses. "They'll fucking kill us, are you fucking insane!"

"Language!" he told his pupil, cringing as he realised how stupid such a demand was on a day like this. Sighing, he gave a shrug. "It's the only thing I can think of. If we can get to the minibus we can drive out of here, it can't be like this all over the island can it?"

"Maybe it is," the voice of Chloe drew his gaze, and he winced at the look of pain on her young face. "Maybe its like this on the mainland too!"

Ian was aghast. "What about my parents?"

"Probably dead," Chloe told him, shrugging as she spoke. "Your dad probably killed your mum, or vice versa, maybe this is how the world is now."

"No!" Ben told her then turned to meet the gaze of each of the other children in turn. "It's not!"

But what if it is true? What do they do then? Oh God, what if she is right?

"Listen to me," Ben stated, unable to see the look of fear in their eyes a moment longer. "I will go and get the minibus. I want you to wait here, OK?"

There was a chorus of concerned mumbling among them and then Chloe raised an eyebrow. "You will come back for us? You promise."

"Of course, he told her, trying to smile in what he hoped was a reassuring manner. "Here take the cleaver. Use it if you need to."

"Won't you need it?" she raised an eyebrow.

Ben forced a smile. "Hopefully not."

He held her gaze a moment longer then turned and began to hurry down the sloping path to the street as quickly as his wounded hip would allow.

His decision to go for the minibus alone had not just been to keep the children safe, though that had been the main reason. Yet he had not wanted them to see the body of Sally Brooks, murdered at the hands of he and the late McKenzie earlier.

It had taken enough for them to trust him.

If they saw her body, saw what they had done to her, then they would never trust him again.

And if he were to somehow get them to safety, then he needed them to trust him implicitly.

In moments, he was at the bottom of the sloping path, and taking a steadying breath, he crossed the empty street towards the car park, his head turning to search for any signs of danger.

There was nothing save for the remaining figures up near the helicopter, but they seemed to caught up in their orgy of death and violence to notice him for the time being.

Knowing it could change at any moment, Ben hurried on, keeping close to the shop fronts as he walked, teeth gritted against the pain of his wound.

Somehow, he reached the car park unharmed, only to pause as he drew near to the minibus, his stomach threatening to empty its contents as he saw the flock of seagulls that were gathered about the body of Sally Brooks. The girl was still under the vehicles nearside front wheel, the bottom half of her body still trapped beneath the vehicles undercarriage, yet the birds had made a feast of her upper half.

As Ben stared on in horror, the large birds, momentarily put on edge by his arrival returned to their meal, and he gagged as he watched one of them fasten its beak to the girls left nipple, pulling back.

The nipple stretched impossibly long, then split as the sharp edges of the beak cut into its rubbery body, and triumphant, the seagull tried to make off with it only for others to attack it at once.

Beaks rose and fell, blood sprayed, and the bird seemed to crumple under the attack, wings folding about it, as the others began to fight for the discarded nipple, another stabbing its beak into her mouth, seeking the meaty goodness of her tongue.

"Get back you horrible cunts!" he suddenly shouted, filled with a mixture of anger and shame, the first at the horror the birds were perpetrated upon the dead girl, the latter at the fact that he was ultimately responsible for it happening.

The birds took flight, happy to squawk and screech until the large angry man was among them, hands and feet lashing out as he shouted in hatred.

They were gone in moments, but only as far as the air, the mass of white bodies screaming their disapproval as he climbed inside the minibus, a sob of horror escaping him as his weight made the vehicle crunch lower into the body of the girl.

Pausing only long enough to see that the birds had already eaten her eyes, Ben slammed the door of the minibus and pushed the keys into the ignition.

The engine fired as he turned them, relief flooding through him, and licking at his dry lips, he put the vehicle into first gear and put his foot down on the accelerator. The minibus groaned, tried to move, but ultimately it stayed where it was, and cursing, Ben opened the drivers window and leaned out to see exactly what the problem was.

His stomach turned over as he saw that it was caught in the body of Sally, and that the wheel was simply turning on the morass of blood, intestines and crushed internal organs beneath its treads.

"Move it!" he roared, leaning back into the vehicle, and putting his foot down. "Move it!"

Without warning, the minibus left Sally behind, the vehicle lurching forward and cursing, ben put it into second gear and turned the wheel, trying to steer it away from driving into the base of the cliff at the rear of the car park. For a moment he thought that he had left it too late but then the old minibus turned, out of the car park onto the adjoining road.

Ben gave a grunt of triumph, then swore aloud as the figure of a naked man suddenly lurched in front of the vehicle, arms hanging limp at his sides, his body a mass of wounds and bloodstains.

He slammed his foot on the brakes, a hand honking wildly on the horn, and at the very last minute the man turned to look at him, one seemingly huge eye staring back through the windscreen at him in terror from a face devoid of ears, nose, and lips.

Ben screamed in terror.

The naked man screamed back, his toothless maw opening wide, his body jerking like a puppet.

Then the speeding minibus struck him hard, throwing the mutilated wretch backwards and the unfortunate man's head seemed to come apart like a ripe watermelon as it struck the road behind him.

Body shaking, mind reeling, Ben sat behind the wheel of the minibus then blinked in shock as he saw the blonde woman walk slowly from an alleyway, an automatic rifle clasped across her naked body.

She paused beside the dead man, dropping to one knee as she reached down with a hand and touched his chest as if mourning a lover, her words reaching Ben through his open window. "You were supposed to be mine…you were suppos…"

She rose quickly, the automatic weapon rising to point at Ben through the windscreen as she snarled in hatred, her eyes bright with fire. "He was mine…he was mine to use and you took him from me…you too him and you have ruined everything!"

ZOE

Coughing slightly, Zoe turned slowly on the spot, her eyes narrowed as she studied the four figures that were seated in a circle about her, each of them naked, each of them tied securely to a wooden chair with wire about their waists, ankles, and wrists.

In the centre of the circle, beside where she was stood staring at her captives, sat the two tables that she and E.V had been tied to earlier that day, and more recently, David. She trembled slightly at the memory of her neighbour, a wave of grief coursing through her only to be replaced with anger as she glanced at the man who had killed him.

The man who had taken everything from her.

Heaving a deep breath, Zoe dropped her gaze to the tables, studying the empty wine bottle that sat upon one, then drifted to the assorted pile of items that she had gathered and placed upon the other, bloodstained carrier bag sitting beside them.

Her eyes drifted down to settle upon the bag, studying the bloodstains about its opening, then she turned back to stare at the man from the minibus.

In the wake of David's death, she had ordered the man, Ben, from the vehicle and directed him back to her apartment at gunpoint, pausing on the way as she made him collect the contents of the bag.

She had stood watching him as he had carried out her instructions, and Zoe had revelled in his pure revulsion as he had tried not to violently vomit.

As the emotion had registered within the blank slate of her soul, she had known instinctively that this man, Ben, was her new ride-or-die.

Was it because he had taken her other fixation from her? Had the fact that she had been unable to finish off David turned her anger upon the man who had taken that opportunity away from her?

She knew that it was wrong, that everything she had done that morning to David had been vile, even in the face of what he had done to her and E.V.

But the apathy had a hold of her soul, and she would do anything to feel, no matter the asking price.

Two women had rushed at Ben as he had been filling the bag for her, their naked bodies sheathed with blood, their breasts lurching like socks filled with jelly, and she had shot them both dead like dogs.

Ben was hers to play with and no-one else's.

"Why are you doing this?" the dark-haired Doctor Kent asked, and Zoe turned to look at her, studying her lean form and large breasts before meeting her gaze again, ignoring her question.

"Why are you here?" she asked her own.

"You captured us…tied us up…" the doctor blinked, head shaking where she was sat beside Ben.

"Why are you here?" Zoe repeated, and as the woman gave a grunt of confusion, Ben grimaced.

"She means with the guns and helicopters."

"Oh?" Doctor Kent nodded, swallowing as she turned back to look at Zoe. "There were riots, people being attacked…we came to help."

"You're not police," Zoe told her, head shaking at the woman. "Police don't come wearing orange chemical suits and carrying automatic weapons. So, who are you?"

"I…I…" the woman began only to flinch as best as she could as Zoe raised the rifle that she still held and pointed it at her face. "OK, please don't shoot me…please…we are government agents, under the provision of Unit 73."

Zoe raised an eyebrow, watching as beside the doctor, Ben shot the woman a look of confusion, his head starting to shake. "Government…what is…"

"Stop talking," Zoe told him, her top lip curling as she turned the gun toward him. "Hush."

He nodded, eyes downcast, and Zoe turned to study the two men who had accompanied the doctor into her apartment, both of them still unconscious.

"So," Zoe looked back at Doctor Kent. "I want to know how the government got here so quickly. When you entered my home earlier, you mentioned taking me in to study as I was infected. Infected with what? What is making me do this?"

For long moments, the dark-haired woman stared back at Zoe in silence, and she could tell that she was considering lying, until with a sigh, she shook her head. "It's 87-91LS."

"What?" Zoe raised an eyebrow, and before her, the doctor looked like she was going to vomit.

"It's a genetically modified virus, officially registered as 87-91LS, but those of us who worked on it called it the Inanis Bug."

"Inanis?" Zoe took a step closer. "Why?"

"Its Latin for empty," Doctor Kent stared up at her, her voice now little more than a whisper. "All of the subjects exposed to it were supposed to be left devoid of all emotions, empty as it were. It was designed to enable soldiers to perform certain duties without the handicap of feeling guilt or regret."

"Handicap of feeling guilt?" Ben muttered in disbelief, only to fall silent as Zoe glanced at him, then turned back to study the bound doctor.

"What went wrong?"

The government agent winced. "It didn't work as intended. It stripped the subjects of all their emotions except those related to their deepest desire. The subjects then pursued that desire with a fanatical zeal, desperate to feel emotion…like a junkie looking for its fix. There were several deaths…the program was shelved."

"And yet I appear to be infected," Zoe told the woman. "How is that possible?"

Again, the doctor studied her for what felt an age, as if wondering if she had already said too much, then she nodded. "There is a man, on the Isle of Wight, a former member of Unit 73. He was a geneticist, the man who designed the original genome that the virus was constructed from…he lives here…"

"And he released it?" Zoe finished for her, nodding as she spoke. "Why would he do that?"

"He hates the government, he feels we didn't give him the recognition he deserves…"
Zoe stared at the woman in silence for almost a minute, her gaze drifting to the two men as they began to stir and then back once again. "Why does it affect men before it affects women?"

"A subtle difference in physiology," the reply came at once. "The first to be affected by 87-91LS are always males who have passed through puberty. Woman are affected a few hours later. The only difference once infection takes place is women seem to retain more rational thought."

"How long does it affect each person?" Zoe asked, suddenly curious. "How long will this last?"

"I'm sorry," Doctor Kent was pale. "It again depends upon the physiology of the individual. But I can tell you that once you have come back down, you cannot be affected by 87-91LS again, even though it remains in the air indefinitely."

"Indefinitely?" Zoe repeated the word. "So, everyone who breathes it will eventually change?"

There was fear in the eyes of the doctor. "It is out there now, controlled by the air currents, going where it will…there is no taking this back. We can't put the genie back in the lamp! We never intended for this to happen. You can't hold us responsible."

Zoe cocked her head to one side. "Do you know what I have been through today?"

"I'm sorry!" Doctor Kent shook her head.

"Here," Zoe threw the rifle to the side onto her sofa and bent to retrieve a chisel and a hammer from the table, then turned back around towards Doctor Kent as she spoke. "Let me show you."

BEN

"Please don't, you don't have to do this!" the dark-haired woman bound to the chair beside Ben sobbed, head shaking as the blonde woman crouched down and placed the head of what looked like a stone chisel against the centre of her left kneecap.

"I don't care," their captor replied. "Isn't that what you scientists wanted? Congratulations."

"No no no don't!" the woman screeched as the blonde raised the hammer over her shoulder, the head of it heavy and square. "No-no-no-no-no-no!"

She screamed as the woman brought the hammer down, the head striking the chisel hard against the doctor's kneecap, and Ben felt his stomach knot in dread as he heard a sickening crack.

Doctor Kent howled piteously, thrashing against the wires securing her to the chair, and forcing himself to look, Ben stared at her knee, fighting the urge to vomit as he saw the crease in the skin, and the two misshapen lumps either side of it.

"Shhhhh!" the blonde soothed her like a mother would a small child, though the sound was dispassionate, monotone. "We've only just begun!"

"No more," the doctor shook her head as their captor moved the chisel to rest against the side of one of the lumps, and Ben watched in dread as she raised the hammer again. "Please, no more…"

The hammer fell once more, and the scream of raw agony that escaped the doctor made Ben release a shaky breath, his mind reeling as he stared down at the ruins of the woman's left kneecap. The raised section that had been struck was now shaped differently, as if the patella had come loose from its groove in the thigh bone, and deep purple bruises were already starting to spread across the area.

As the blonde woman sat back on her heels, and the doctor sobbed in agony, Ben stared past the pair, watching as the two naked men began to rouse themselves from the sleep that they had been in.

They, and the doctor had all been unconscious when he had arrived at the apartment, forced by the blonde woman with the automatic rifle, and under her direction, he had stripped the three and lifted them to the chairs, then bound them with the wire.

She had then forced him to sit in the fourth chair and bind his own ankles before she had secured him further to the chair about the waist and wrists.

With a groan, the taller of the two men lifted his head from where it had been slumped forwards, his hard, almost square features turning to study Ben, and the two women, his lips moving silently.

Their captor turned towards him at the sudden movement and rising to her feet, she had cast the chisel and hammer to the tables and studied him intently for a moment before speaking. "Don't ask any questions…you are my guests…my name is Zoe…that's all you need to know."

"Guests…" the man repeated her words, a look of recognition creeping onto his cruel face as he stared back at her. "You knocked me out!"

The woman, Zoe, stayed quiet and Ben felt his soul shrivel as he saw the dead eyes of the man staring at her, realising in that instant that he was under the influence of the mysterious 87-91LS. As if in a daze, the man turned his gaze to the stirring man beside him, then to Ben and finally to the doctor, a spark of excitement finally registering upon his features. "Well, well, well Doctor Cunt…"

Before Ben, Zoe seemed to have noticed the man's behaviour too, and she licked at her lips, glancing at the doctor before looking back at the big man. "Jenkins…"

"Let me out of this chair," the man told Zoe, his eyes never leaving the sobbing female doctor.

"And if I do? What then?" Zoe raised an eyebrow. "What will you do? Try and kill me?"

"Not straight away," the man told her honestly, meeting her gaze briefly before looking back at the doctor. "First I'm gonna fuck that bitch."

"Jenkins!" the doctor gasped, a look of shock upon her face as she turned to stare at him. "How dare you…"

"Shut your mouth," he told her, a sneer on his features as he studied her. "Ordering me about, talking down to me…you've had it coming for a long time, cunt, and you are gonna get yours!"

"So exciting," Zoe stated, and Ben felt the hairs on his arms stand on end as she nodded. "I think I might let you out of that chair after all."

"No!" the doctor sobbed. "No please!"

"Do it," the big man tensed in his chair and Ben forced himself to look away as he saw the man's thick cock hardening as he stared over at the doctor.

"First things first," Zoe bent and picked up a small pair of wire cutters and moved to his chair. As Ben watched in disbelief, she cut through most of the wires about one wrist and then placed the cutters on his lap before stepping towards the sofa and scooping the automatic rifle up into her hands again.

Moving back slightly, she nodded at the man, Jenkins. "Free yourself. Go on."

With a cold chuckle, he strained his right wrist, bending the single wire that still secured his hand, and slipped it out. Picking up the cutters, he cut his other wrist free, then his waist, and then his ankles.

The doctor gave a shriek of terror as he suddenly slid from his chair and stepped over to her, one hand wrapping tight in her hair while his other reached down to maul at her breasts. "Bitch..."

"Leave her alone!" Ben snapped, then gasped in pain as the man turned, his hand leaving the doctors breasts to punch him hard on the nose. He felt the cartilage break under the impact, bright light flashing through his eyes as the pain shot through his face, blood running from his broken nose.

"Stop!" the voice of Zoe made the big man pause as he raised his fist to punch Ben a second time. "You do what I tell you or you get shot!"

"I'm gonna fuck you too, cunt!" Jenkins turned to stare at her coldly, and Ben felt like he had a thousand spiders in his hair as he saw the madness in Zoe's eyes as she stared back at the large man.

"Spin the bottle."

Jenkins grunted, and she repeated herself, nodding towards the empty wine bottle on the table.

Jenkins grinned coldly. "How about I break it over your head and fuck your arse with it!"

"Spin the bottle!" Zoe took a step closer and for a moment, Ben thought that Jenkins might try and rush her. But then the big man nodded and bent, his right hand spinning the bottle on the small table. Round and round it went, and seated beside the doctor, Ben found himself struggling to stay calm as the bottle began to slow, its inertia fading away. He grunted in denial as the bottle looked as though it would end with the neck pointing towards him but then it wibbled on and came to rest facing the unconscious man on the other side of the doctor.

"Well?" Jenkins turned to stare back at Zoe.

She hesitated, her gaze drifting to Ben before she looked back at the large figure of Jenkins. "I want you to break his fingers, all of them."

Without even hesitating, Jenkins turned and moved to crouch beside the chair with the other man, his hands reaching out and despite not wanting to, Ben found himself watching in grim fascination.

There was a sharp crunching crack, and the man in the chair awoke with a scream of pain, his eyes wide in his face, as Jenkins laughed softly and calmly broke another finger. The man gave another scream, shorter now, his nostrils flaring as he tried to breathe through the pain. Mind reeling, Ben watched as Jenkins worked his way along the rest of the man's hand then moved to the other, though as he went on the man gave less reaction to the breaks.

"Having fun, Watson?" Jenkins asked calmly as he broke the last finger and rose to step away.

Watson lifted his head to stare back at his attacked, the corner of his mouth twitching into a smile. "I fucking hate you, you Welsh cunt."

Ben blinked in disbelief, stunned at how well the man Watson was taking his injuries. Had he seemed as able to stand injury when he had been infected hours ago? He tried to think back, recalling that Abby had cut the bridge of his nose with her knife as he had been attacking her but nothing more.

Abby.

He fought to keep the moan of grief from escaping him as he recalled his murder of the woman that he had loved, only aware that the bottle was spinning once more when Doctor Kent began to sob beside him. "Not me not me not me not me!"

"Ben!" Zoe exclaimed with an almost lustful gasp and despite himself, he let out whine as he saw the bottle stop facing him, his body going rigid.

Jenkins glanced towards Zoe, awaiting instructions, and she pursed her lips, her eyes flicking to the pile of items upon the table and then about the room. "What to do…what to do…ah yes."

"No!" Ben gasped, not even knowing what it was that she had planned for him. "Don't do it!"

"Bring me one of the dogs eyes," Zoe told Jenkins, and he turned and moved over to the animal which lay on its side beside the wall where she had told Ben to drag it while setting the room up earlier. Ben flinched as he heard the wet noises coming from the dog as Jenkins crouched beside it, the man's bored voice reaching back to where he sat. "Slippery bugger…ah, here we go!"

He turned, one palm extended, and Ben gagged as he saw the eyeball resting on it, congealed blood and tissue coating the off-white veiny orb, the black iris and the pupil at its centre seeming large.

"Make him eat it," Zoe stated calmly, and Ben felt a pain in his neck as he jerked his head towards her in shock, fighting the urge to vomit at her words.

"No, I'll do anything you want…please."

"I want you to eat the eye!" she replied, gun pointing at him, and he gave a choking sob of denial.

"Shoot me…get it over with! I won't do it!"

"Make him," Zoe turned the gun back upon Jenkins and he nodded, stepping over towards Ben.

"Fuck you!" he shouted at him, struggling against his bonds. "Get the fuck away from m…"

Ben was still shouting when the man grasped him in a headlock with one arm, the other palming the large eyeball into his gaping mouth. Ben screeched against the hand over his lips, his stomach starting to churn as he felt the cold sticky orb inside his mouth, his tongue curling as he tried to move it away. His throat tightened with the promise of vomit as his teeth brushed against the orb, Ben's nostrils flaring, his own eyes wide as he felt a slimy coating slide off from it and slither down his throat like an oyster.

Muscles bunching, Ben tried to rise, feeling the pain of the wire cutting into his wrists as he thrashed about, trying to scream his anger and disgust. His back teeth caught the eye as it rolled, crunching into its jelly-like surface and like a spot popping, acrid fluid filled Ben's mouth, the tissue of the orb slipping about among it like the fat skin of a grape.

"Swallow it like a good boy!" Zoe told him, and without being told to, Jenkins pinched his nostrils together, cutting off the only air supply that he had.

Eyes filled with tears, Ben held on for as long as he could, his lungs burning, his mouth filled with the crushed and jellified ruins of the dogs eyeball until he was forced to swallow it down in one go.

Without warning, Jenkins released him and stepped back, and Ben sucked great lungful's of air in his body, his vision blurry with the tears in his eyes.

"Spin the bottle!" Zoe instructed, and Ben shook his head weakly, while Doctor Kent began to sob once more, her body shaking with the exertion.

Round and round it span, wobbling slightly as it went, and Ben found himself willing it to stop on the man Watson, rather than himself or the doctor.

He roared in denial as it came to rest upon him once more, teeth gritting as he stared at Zoe, and she chuckled in what seemed genuine pleasure as she addressed Jenkins. "I think he is still hungry. Find him something else to eat from the dog."

"Fuck you!" Ben shouted, knowing that it wasn't her fault but still hating her for her actions. Jenkins nodded, turned to head to the dog once more, and Ben shook his head as wet noise began once more, chest heaving in dread of what lay ahead.

With a grunt of triumph, Jenkins turned back to face Ben, his grisly prize clasped tight in his bloody fingers, yet it was Doctor Kent who cried out in horror and disgust, her head shaking in denial.

"Perfect," Zoe smiled, her eyes meeting those of Ben as he glanced at her, and then he turned back to the naked man that was approaching him, his gaze dropping to stare in horror at the dogs tongue that Jenkins had torn from the mouth of the animal.

The man continued towards him, waggling the long purple strip of meat in his hand, like a ham insole, muscle and tissue hanging from the back of the tongue where it had been violently torn free.

Desperately Ben tried to move his head back away, but it was no use. With quick movements, the big man stepped up to him, thrusting two fingers into his nostrils and yanking his head back. Gasping in pain, Ben found himself staring up at the ceiling, neck aching at the angle he had been forced into and he opened his mouth to scream in agony only to gag as Jenkins lowered the tongue between his lips.

Try as he might, Ben couldn't expel the foreign body from his mouth, his own tongue swirling frantically as he tried to use it as a lever, and he nearly shrieked in insanity as he realised that he was effectively French kissing a dead dog.

"Bite it," Zoe told him. "One bite, that's all."

Ben tried to scream, the sound that escaped his mouth akin to the gargling yodel of a porn star trying to talk around a cock in her mouth, and in desperation he clamped his teeth together tight.

The meat quivered as he bit it, chewier than he had expected, the cold touch of the slimy flesh making him his gag reflex activate. Tears filling his eyes, Ben worked his teeth harder, shaking his head from side like a dog trying to kill a rat, his nostrils still crammed full of Jenkin's stinking fingers.

Without warning the bottom section of tongue came loose, dropping into his mouth, and Ben nearly shrieked as it plopped against the roof of his mouth, threatening to fall and block his throat.

Mind threatening to unravel, he jerked his head, knocking it back towards his teeth as Jenkins cast aside the rest of the tongue and clamped his hand over Ben's mouth, watching silently as the teacher was forced to chew the tongue into pieces.

97

ZOE

Leaning back against the wall of her living room, the automatic rifle clasped in her hands, Zoe watched the man who had killed David with excitement as he choked and gagged, each small expression of pain or discomfort making her quake with passion.

She frowned as she considered her reasons for bringing him here, her brow furrowing as she realised that she could no long picture David, and that realisation made her breath catch in her throat.

Not that she had loved David, no, far from it, yet he had been hers to do as she saw fit with.

And now he had been taken from her by this man. This Ben Grass. This eater of eyes and tongues.

She chuckled, drawing the gaze of Jenkins and she nodded at him, telling him to spin the bottle again, and sneering at her, he did as instructed.

Adjusting her grip on the automatic rifle, Zoe studied the broad back of the man Jenkins, knowing that he was going to violently rape, torture and kill her the moment that she lowered her guard.

Problems for a later date.

The bottle finally came to a halt on Watson, and he lifted his gaze to meet that of Jenkin's, and then her. "Go on then."

Intrigued, she took a step forward, her own eyebrow lifting. "What do you want?"

"I want to kill you."

"No," she shook her head, seeing the bored expression on his face. "What do you really want…more than anything."

He licked at his lips, his gaze drifting sideways to settle upon Ben, a sudden spark of excitement seeming to register on his face. "I want him…I want to use every hole he has and then I want to make new ones so I can fuck them too!"

"No!" Ben's gasp was one of horror, and Zoe fought the jealousy and excitement that coursed through her, each vying for supremacy.

"What am I doing with him?" the voice of Jenkins asked, the tone devoid of all emotion even though Watson was his colleague. "Well?"

"The kitchen fork," she nodded at the items on the small table. "Stab him with it."

"How long for?"

"Until I tell you to stop."

He grunted and bent to retrieve the long metal form, holding it before him like a Roman gladius as he approached his colleague. "Nothing personal."

"Fuck you," Watson told him almost calmly.

"Fuck you," Jenkins nodded, then stabbed him hard in the chest with the makeshift weapon. Watson tensed, hissing in pain, and Jenkins stabbed him again, then three more times in quick succession, each of the wounds from the two-pronged fork bleeding as he had been bitten by a vampire.

Teeth gritted, Watson raised his gaze to meet that of his colleague as Jenkins continued to stab him, the chest and stomach of the former awash with blood until finally Zoe sighed. "Enough. Spin the bottle again."

Once more it span, round and around, and Zoe turned to study the man Ben, enjoying the look of terror and dread upon his face as he watched it as it stopped pointing towards him for the third time.

"And?" Jenkins asked her, taking a step in the direction of the dog. "What is he eating now?"

"Nothing from the dog," she told him, fighting to stop from shuddering as she spoke, her eyes drifting to settle upon the bloody carrier bag.

As she lifted her gaze she saw Ben watching her in terror, his mouth trembling and she nearly swooned at the emotion if sent through her body.

After all, Ben knew exactly what was in the bag, having been made to collect it earlier by Zoe.

"Open the bag," she told Jenkins. "Fold it back so we can all see what's inside."

The big man nodded, then stepped to the bag, and opened it wide. For a moment, the large man stared down inside its depths then he glanced up at her. "Is this…?"

"Open the bag wide, Ben is hungry."

He screamed at her words, rocking back and forth on his chair as Jenkins did as instructed, slowly opening the bag until it resembled a plastic plate, almost overflowing with its foul-smelling contents.

"Make him eat it!" she told Jenkins, and nodding, he turned back to meet the gaze of Ben.

"Dinners ready."

The other man screamed in denial, his chair rocking once more, and grimacing, Jenkins grabbed the back of the chair and dragged it to the table. As Zoe watched, the big man took a step back as if judging the distance, then grabbed the chair and tipped it forward, dropping Ben face first into it.

The pile of afterbirth, freshly scooped from the husk of the woman that Zoe had found outside a gift shop, seemed to wrap about the face of Ben like an over-friendly octopus, and he screamed into it, the sound muffled and choked, as if he were eating.

Which he was.

"Lift him," Zoe instructed Jenkins, and the man dragged back on the chair, lifting Ben several inches from the quivering mass of human waste. He glanced up at her, gasping for air, his lips and nose bloody, and what looked like jelly-like membrane attaching him to the afterbirth like jellyfish tentacles.

"Down," she told Jenkins, and he nodded, pushing the chair so that Ben's face plunged back into the foul morass. It seemed to come part under the sudden impact; blood and foetal membrane exploding all over the face of the choking man.

For some time, Zoe watched him struggling in the pile of organs and blood, his muffled screams faint until she sighed and gestured Jenkins to lift him and drag him back. The man did as instructed, and she licked at her lips as she saw the gore on the face of Ben and the unhinged look of horror in his eyes.

"Spin the bottle again," Zoe told Jenkins as he stepped back before the chairs, and he did just that.

It stopped on Doctor Kent, and almost at once, the woman began to sob and whine, pleading for mercy while beside her, Ben looked down, but not before Zoe saw the relief upon his features.

"Give her to me, let me fuck the cunt!" the snarl of Jenkins was full of lust and excitement.

"Not yet!" Zoe told him then turned to the doctor, watching as the woman fought to compose herself. "How old are you…tell me."

"I'm thirty…thirty-six."

"The drill," Zoe nodded to the handheld power drill on the table as Jenkins glanced at her, a slender drill bit fitted to it. "I want you to drill into her thirty-six times."

"Where?" the big man picked up the drill, watching as he pressed the button, and it span with a buzzing whirr of metal. "The eyes?"

"No," Zoe mused. "The soles of her feet."

Doctor Kent began to screech, jerking wildly against the wire around her ankles as Jenkins knelt before her, and untied one of them. Intrigued, Zoe watched as he lifted her leg straight out before her, clamping it tight under his arm as he brought the buzzing drill towards the soft sole of her left foot.

"No!" she screamed, toes flexing as if that might somehow keep the drill away from her foot.

"Are you ready?" Jenkins turned to look at her, and though Zoe couldn't see his face, she could hear the lust in his voice. "You hear me you beautiful bitch, this is just the fucking start!"

With a chuckle, he slowly dragged the whirling drill bit but up the sole, barely touching and the woman gave a strange shudder at the sensation. Then he pushed the drill bit into her foot, and Zoe watched as her toes all splayed out as if they were shocked by-standers…five bald little dwarves horrified by what they were witnessing.

"Two…three….four…" Jenkins counted aloud as he pushed the drill back and forth into the crinkled, softness of her foot, deliberately avoiding the heel end and aiming for halfway towards the toes.

"Sixteen…seventeen…eighteen," Jenkins suddenly bent and ran the flat blade of his tongue up the bleeding sole of Doctor Kent's foot, drawing an agonized howl of disgust from her. Chuckling, he reached down to unfasten her right foot, raising her leg up high as he had her left then he picked the drill back up. "Just another eighteen to go, little whore."

She screeched as he began to drill into her once more, and Zoe watched with genuine interest, occasionally letting her gaze drift over towards Ben.

He was watching too, shame on his pale face, and in that moment Zoe watched to hurt him so bad that she felt her body tremble with the intensity.

"Thirty-four…thirty-five…thirty-six," Jenkins released her foot to bump from the floor, drawing a sobbing moan from the doctor as she sat half slumped in the chair, the wire about her waist and her wrists the only things keeping her upright.

"Spin the bottle," Zoe instructed Jenkins, and he cast a look back at her, a dark expression upon his features as he reached down and took his hard cock into his hands, the fingers gliding back and forth.

"I don't think so!"

Zoe adjusted her grip on the rifle as she stared at him, ready to shoot him should he move for her but then without warning he was reaching for the figure of Doctor Kent, hands pulling at her bonds.

"No, get your hands off me!" she screamed, eyes wide in her face, the pain in her feet forgotten in the face of what he clearly had planned for her.

"Cunt!" he backhanded her across the face, then turned to grin at Ben as he began to shout for him to stop. "Keep your mouth shut pretty boy or I'll do you next!"

"He's mine!" Watson was sudden animated, fighting to get out of his chair and Zoe moaned softly as she saw the fear upon the face of Ben.

Smirking, Jenkins turned back to glance at Zoe, saw that she wasn't about to gun him down then continued to pull the wire from the doctor. With a snarl, he dragged her from the chair, lifting her smaller frame as if she weighed nothing at all. She grunted in shock as he dropped her down onto an armchair on the other side of Ben, her legs raised high over his broad shoulders, and Zoe watched as his thick cock hung down, the meaty arrowhead pointing at the woman's splayed open vagina.

"Are you ready you gorgeous cunt?" Jenkins snarled at his victim. "Here comes the pain!"

"Please…please!" she sobbed, her chest heaving, and Jenkins chuckled and moved his legs lower so that the swollen head of his circumcised cock pushed gently against her as if nuzzling in.

"Beg me," he snarled, his voice throaty, one hand reaching down to violently maul at her breasts as if kneading dough. "Beg me like the whore you."

"Oh please, please don't hurt me!"

"I like your tears," he grunted as he pushed into her, and Zoe watched mesmerised as above his shoulders, the toes of her bleeding feet curled, a drawn-out animal moan escaping the doctor.

Stepping closer, Zoe studied the thick shape of his cock as it sank into the soft pliable flesh of his victim, then pulled almost all the way back out before plunging back down into her, deeper than before. Doctor Kent groaned aloud and dropping to his knees before her, Jenkins dragged her with him to lay on the edge of the armchairs cushion, one big hand grasping painfully to a breast, his other fastening about her throat as he fucked her hard.

Time lost all meaning to Zoe as she watched the show, while before her Jenkins suddenly pulled out and flipped his victim over so that she was bent over the cushion, large breasts squished against it.

With a sneer, Jenkins rose to squat above her, the base of his shiny erection clasped in a hand as he pushed it against her arsehole, his other hand reaching about to clutch at the front of her throat, pulling back on her so that she began to choke.

He moved his hips, his hand pushing his hard cock at his victims arsehole, and for a moment there was resistance, his cock bending slightly. Snarling, he spat on it, his fingers coating his shaft and without warning it pushed inside her. Doctor Kent went stiff, mouth opening and closing silently, and pushing down in the small of her back with a hand, Jenkins transferred his other from her throat to her long hair, grunting and muttering obscenities as he raped her.

Watching, Zoe found herself smiling as she saw Ben's discomfort and horror, every look of anguish sending jolts of raw emotion through her.

This was everything. This was heaven.

This was wrong…

The realness of what she was orchestrating registered in her with the force of a shotgun to the synapses, shame and grief swamping her.

What was she doing? What was she doing!

With a roar, Jenkin's suddenly pushed deep inside his victim as he came hard, dragging the doctor back against his body as he sucked on the side of her neck, his hands groping at her breasts once more as he sneered. "Now you can suck it dr…"

He was still talking when Zoe stepped closer and shot him in the head, the bullet seeming to disintegrate the back of the large man's skull.

Doctor Kent gasped at the gunfire, and as the big man collapsed as if his strings had been cut, she was dragged down with him, his cock still embedded deep inside her arsehole, while Ben sat screaming in shock, face and mouth caked in blood and brains.

"What the fuck!" he screamed, eyes appearing extra white against the gore coating his face and she held his gaze for a moment then turned to Watson.

"Do you want to fuck him?"

Watson's face lit up with excitement, a cruel smile appearing on his face as he looked hungrily over at Ben. "Untie me and I'll fucking ruin him…"

Zoe shot him in the face, the force of the weapon throwing his chair backwards to the floor.

For what felt an eternity, she stood staring down at the body of the man that she had just executed, tears stinging her eyes as she considered all that she had done. Then she turned back to study the bloody face of Ben, and the sobbing Doctor Kent as she tried to rise, her voice breaking as she spoke. "I am so sorry…"

BEN

"Where did you leave them?" Zoe asked Ben as they drove slowly along the deserted seafront, seated in the passenger seat in the front of the minibus.

He forced himself to glance at her, fighting away the wave of anger that coursed through him at the memory of the things that she had done to him within the last hour. After all, he had done far worse.

He had murdered his pupils.

"Up there," he nodded, as he steered around a body lying naked and face-down in the road, making sure not to study it too closely. "Near the woodland place with the dinosaurs."

"The Chine," she nodded, and he forced a smile as he met her gaze, knowing in that moment he had already forgiven her for what had happened.

A sob from the rear of the minibus made him glance in his rear-view mirror, his stomach knotting as he saw the pale features of Doctor Kent, her intense gaze locked to the back of Zoe's head.

Not everyone was going to forgive so easily.

Gritting his teeth, fighting the urge to vomit as he recalled all the things that had been in his mouth within the last hour, Ben drove onwards, eyes narrowing as he looked for any sign of his pupils.

Had they thought he had abandoned them?

It wouldn't surprise him if so.

Damn it.

If he hadn't run that man down.

"Who was he?" he asked suddenly, gaze shifting to Zoe before turning back to the road. "The man that I killed…a boyfriend…a brother?"

"My neighbour," she replied, head shaking in his peripheral vision. "The things I made you do…"

"Weren't your fault," he told her, hoping that he sounded convincing, his own guilt surfacing again.

They drove on for a minute in silence, then pulled up at the base of the sloping path towards the Chine, the last place that Ben had seen the children.

"So where are they?" Zoe asked again, and he gave a shrug, swinging open his door and getting out.

He winced as pain in his hip resurfaced, the wound momentarily forgotten in the wake of the hours under Zoe's control. Slamming his door, he moved to the front of the vehicle, then turning to watch as Zoe called out for him to wait as she exited the vehicle and moved to him. "Where are they?"

"I don't know," he told her as they began to walk side-by-side, concern surfacing in him again as he pictured his charges. "I hope they are OK."

She forced a smile, a hand brushing her hair behind an ear as she nodded. "I am sure that…"

They both span about as the scream of horror and agony sounded, each of them taking a step back as they saw the five teenagers dragging the sobbing figure of Doctor Kent from the minibus to the ground. The screaming woman tried to rise then fell to her back; Jessie, Lisa, and Ian stabbing at her with knives while Chloe hacked into her throat with the cleaver that Ben had given her to look after, blood spurting freely as the doctors head came free.

As one, the four children rose and moved to stand in a line across the bottom of the sloping path, and fighting the twisting in his gut, Ben looked at Zoe. "Run!"

About the Author

Born in Portsmouth, England in 1973, Kelvin V.A Allison has somehow found his way to the hill strewn paradise that is County Durham, where he lives a life of calm and insanity in equal measure in the village home that he shares with his fiancée, and their four children.

An author of over fifty novels, including the ten book World of Sorrow series, he is also an avid board gamer, and a lifetime fan of fruit filled sugared pastries. He would prefer it if you did not judge him.